Who Walked with the Walkie-talkie?

"Bess?" Nancy asked slowly. "What happened to my walkie-talkie?"

"I wish I knew!" Bess wailed. "I . . . lost it!"

"You lost my walkie-talkie?" Nancy gasped. She could feel her heart pounding.

"I raced the boys to the ice-cream truck," Bess explained. "I was the first in line. But when Mr. Swirly Head held out my cone, I needed two hands to take it."

"So you put down Nancy's walkie-talkie?" George asked. "Where?"

"On the ledge outside the truck window," Bess explained. "I turned away for only a few seconds. But when I reached for the walkie-talkie—it was gone!"

The Nancy Drew Notebooks

Available from MINSTREL Books

THE
NANCY DREW
NOTEBOOKS®

#43

The Walkie-talkie Mystery

CAROLYN KEENE
ILLUSTRATED BY JAN NAIMO JONES

A MINSTREL®
BOOK

Published by POCKET BOOKS
New York   London   Toronto   Sydney   Singapore

This book is a work of fiction. Names, characters, places and incidents are products of the author's imagination or are used fictitiously. Any resemblance to actual events or locales or persons living or dead is entirely coincidental.

A MINSTREL PAPERBACK *Original*

 A Minstrel Book published by
POCKET BOOKS, a division of Simon & Schuster, Inc.
1230 Avenue of the Americas, New York, NY 10020

ISBN: 0-7434-0691-5

First Minstrel Books printing August 2001

10 9 8 7 6 5 4 3 2 1

NANCY DREW, THE NANCY DREW NOTEBOOKS, A MINSTREL BOOK and colophon are registered trademarks of Simon & Schuster, Inc.

Cover art by Joanie Schwarz

Printed in the U.S.A.

PHX/

The Walkie-talkie Mystery

1

Over and Out —and Gone!

I'll give you a hint," eight-year-old Nancy Drew said. "It comes in a set. And it's smaller than a lunchbox."

"Golf clubs!" Bess Marvin guessed.

Bess's cousin George Fayne rolled her dark eyes. "Bess!" she said. "Golf clubs aren't smaller than a lunchbox!"

"Okay, then," Bess said, her blue eyes lighting up. *Miniature* golf clubs!"

Nancy laughed. It was Wednesday afternoon. Her best friends, Bess and George, were trying to guess what she had in the shopping bag.

"Time's up," Nancy said. She reached into the small shopping bag and pulled out two hot-green gadgets.

They were shaped like small radios. Each had buttons, dials, and a green antenna. They looked exactly the same.

"What are they?" George asked.

"They're walkie-talkies," Nancy said excitedly. "If I speak into one walkie-talkie, then the person with the other can hear me up to two miles away."

"Two miles!" George exclaimed. "Are you going to use them when you solve your mysteries, Nancy?"

Nancy shook her head. She loved solving mysteries. She even had a blue detective notebook where she wrote her suspects and clues. But the walkie-talkies were for a different reason.

"My father wants us to use them in crowded places," Nancy said. "In case we get separated. Or lost."

"I wish I had a walkie-talkie," George said. "Then if I got lost in the mall, my mom would know where to find me."

"Everyone knows where to find *you,*

George," Bess joked. "In the sports store."

"Ha, ha," George said. She twirled the soccer whistle around her neck.

"Daddy and I are going to use them in the mall this Saturday," Nancy said. "When I go shopping for back-to-school clothes."

"School?" George cried. "It's only the middle of August. We still have three weeks, six days, and sixteen hours to go."

Nancy began to put the walkie-talkies back in the shopping bag.

"Don't put them away yet," Bess said. "Not before we play with them."

"Can't," Nancy said. "My dad said that the walkie-talkies aren't a toy."

"We wouldn't *really* be playing with them," George said. "Just giving them a test run."

Nancy had already tested her walkie-talkies with her dad. But she still wanted to show her friends how they worked.

"Okay," Nancy said. "But we have to be very careful."

The girls walked out of the Drews' yard onto the sidewalk. Nancy set both walkie-talkies to the same channel.

She was about to hand one to Bess when she heard someone yell:

"BEEP! BEEP!"

Nancy looked up. Jason Hutchings and Mike Minelli were riding up her block on silver scooters.

"Pests on wheels," George groaned.

Nancy wondered where David Berger was. The three boys were in the girls' third-grade class. They were always together.

"Nyah, nyah!" Jason sneered. "We have new scooters and you don't!"

"So what?" George called. "Nancy has new walkie-talkies and you don't!"

Nancy froze as the boys screeched to a stop. Did George have to tell the boys?

"Cool!" Mike exclaimed.

"*Totally* cool!" Jason gasped. "Those have to be the new *Moleheads from Mars* Space Patrol Radios."

"They're not," Nancy said. She knew that *Moleheads from Mars* was the boys' favorite TV show.

"And speaking of space cadets," George said, "where's David?"

4

"His mom took him shopping for school supplies." Jason sighed. "Poor guy."

Mike snickered. Then he grabbed a walkie-talkie right out of Nancy's hand.

"Mission control to spaceship," Mike called into the walkie-talkie. "The space aliens have landed. And they want pizza."

"Give it back!" Nancy demanded.

"You want it?" Mike asked. He began scooting away with Jason. "Come get it!"

Nancy froze. The boys were speeding up the block—with her walkie-talkie!

"Bess, George!" Nancy cried. "I have to get it back!"

The girls chased the boys, but they couldn't catch them.

"Nancy!" George shouted. "Give me your other walkie-talkie. Quick!"

"Why?" Nancy asked. She stopped running and gave George her walkie-talkie.

George grabbed her soccer whistle. She blasted it into the walkie-talkie.

TWEEEEEEEEE!!!

"Yow!" Mike yelped. He stumbled off his scooter and dropped Nancy's walkie-talkie onto the grass.

"Gotcha!" Nancy said. She grabbed her walkie-talkie.

"We were just playing space games," Mike complained.

"Then why don't you do us a favor and blast off?" George joked.

Nancy shook her head as Jason and Mike scooted around the corner.

"Now let's play—I mean—test out my walkie-talkies," Nancy said. She handed one to Bess.

"What do I do?" Bess asked.

"Go around the corner," Nancy said. "Then hold down the black button and speak into the walkie-talkie. I'll answer back."

"Neat!" Bess said excitedly. "I'll tell you a funny joke."

Bess ran around the corner. Nancy counted slowly to ten. Then she spoke into the walkie-talkie.

"Bess?" she asked. "Can you read me?"

"Not unless you're a book," Bess's voice answered. "Knock, knock."

"Who's there?" Nancy asked.

"Mr. Swirly Head!" Bess shouted.

"Mr. Swirly Head who?" Nancy asked.

"No," Bess answered. "The Mr. Swirly Head ice-cream truck is coming."

Nancy could hear the Mr. Swirly Head music jingle through her walkie-talkie.

"I can't talk when my mouth is watering!" Bess cried. "Over and out!"

Nancy heard a click.

"What do you expect?" George sighed. "Bess drops everything for ice cream."

"I just hope she doesn't drop my walkie-talkie," Nancy joked.

She couldn't blame Bess. Mr. Swirly Head sold the most awesome ice cream. His Skyscraper cones were so high that you had to stand on your toes to lick them.

Mr. Swirly Head even wore a plastic swirled ice-cream hat on his head. It made him look like a giant ice-cream cone.

Nancy wanted ice cream, too. But when she looked at her watch, it was 4:30 — too close to dinnertime.

"We'd better go around the corner and help Bess," Nancy said. "No way she can hold a Skyscraper and my walkie-talkie at the same time."

But just as Nancy was about to turn the corner, she saw Bess. She was walking down the block with a Skyscraper cone in her hand.

Her face was chalk white, and strawberry ice cream was dripping down her arm.

"Bess?" Nancy asked slowly. "What happened to my walkie-talkie?"

"I wish I knew!" Bess wailed. "I . . . lost it!"

2

Mean, Green—and Seen

You lost my walkie-talkie?" Nancy gasped. She could feel her heart pounding.

"I raced the boys to the ice-cream truck," Bess explained. "I was the first in line. But when Mr. Swirly Head held out my cone, I needed two hands to take it."

"So you put down Nancy's walkie-talkie?" George asked. "Where?"

"On the ledge outside the truck window," Bess explained. "I turned away for only a few seconds. But when I reached for the walkie-talkie—it was gone!"

Gone! The word hit Nancy like a ton of

bricks. How was she ever going to explain this to her father?

"I tried to ask the other kids if they'd seen it," Bess went on. "But they were pushing past me to buy ice cream."

"What about the boys?" Nancy asked. "What were they doing?"

"Jason and Mike were scooting away," Bess said. "They didn't even have ice-cream cones."

Nancy could tell Bess was upset. She was dripping strawberry ice cream all over her new blouse, and she didn't even care.

"Maybe the walkie-talkie fell on the ground," George suggested.

Bess pointed to her dirty knees. "I looked there, too!" she wailed. "I looked everywhere!"

"Unless it fell the other way," Nancy said. "*Inside* the truck."

"Let's check it out!" George cried.

The girls darted around the corner. The ice-cream truck was still there.

Nancy saw Mr. Swirly Head lean out of the truck window. He was wearing his usual bright pink swirly hat.

11

"What can I get for you girls?" Mr. Swirly Head asked with a smile.

"A walkie-talkie," Bess said quickly.

"Walkie-talkie?" Mr. Swirly Head asked. He shook his head. "I've got ice-cream bars but not walkie-talkies."

Nancy pulled out her other walkie-talkie. She showed it to Mr. Swirly Head.

"It's a *real* walkie-talkie," Nancy said. "It looks just like this one."

"I lost it when I bought a Skyscraper," Bess said. "Did you find it?"

Mr. Swirly Head looked down at the floor of the truck. Then he called over his shoulder.

"Hey, Ethan?" Mr. Swirly Head asked. "Did you find a walkie-talkie?"

Nancy watched as a boy peeked out from behind a tower of cardboard boxes. He was holding a book about dinosaurs and wearing a bright blue swirly hat.

"No," Ethan said. He looked through a box marked Lost and Found. "Just a Frisbee and some kid's retainer. Too gross!"

Nancy recognized the boy. He was Ethan Taylor from the second grade.

12

"I didn't know your dad was Mr. Swirly Head," Nancy said to Ethan.

Ethan nodded. "Dad asked me to help after camp ended. I'm going to pitch in three days a week!" he said proudly.

"Ethan is a chip off the old block," Mr. Swirly Head joked. He pointed to the freezer. "The ice block. Get it?"

"Da-ad!" Ethan groaned, turning red.

Nancy was too worried to laugh. Her walkie-talkie was nowhere to be found.

"I'm sorry, Nancy," Bess said sadly.

"Nancy?" Ethan repeated. "I knew it!"

"Knew what?" Nancy asked.

"You're Nancy Drew, the school detective," Ethan said. "I heard you're good."

"The best," George bragged.

"Thanks." Nancy sighed. She placed her walkie-talkie into her pocket. "I hope I'm good enough to find my walkie-talkie."

George bought a chocolate Skyscraper. Then the girls walked back to Nancy's house.

"I think someone *took* my walkie-talkie," Nancy declared.

"Who?" Bess asked. She popped the last of her cone into her mouth.

"That's what I'm going to find out," Nancy said. She ran into the house. In a flash she was outside with her blue detective notebook and a pencil.

The girls sat down on the Drews' doorstep. Bess and George looked over Nancy's shoulder as she opened her notebook to a fresh page.

On the top of the page she wrote, "Where's my walkie-talkie?"

First Nancy wrote that the walkie-talkie was taken on Wednesday at 4:30. She knew because she had looked at her watch.

Then she skipped two lines and wrote the word "suspects."

"Jason and Mike were behind Bess in the ice-cream line," Nancy said. "And they ran away *without* any ice cream."

George narrowed her eyes. "No one leaves Mr. Swirly Head without ice cream."

Nancy wrote the boys' names in her notebook. Then she turned to Bess.

"Who else did you see in the ice-cream line?" Nancy asked.

Bess scrunched her nose. "I think I saw Andrew Leoni. But I'm not sure."

Nancy nodded. Andrew was in the girls' third-grade class.

"Aha!" George said. "I'll bet Andrew did it!"

"Why?" Nancy asked.

"Don't you remember?" George asked. "Andrew once took your pen-pal letters in school just so he could have the stamps. Once a sneak, always a sneak!"

Nancy shook her head. "Andrew was very sorry about taking my letters," she said. "I don't think he'd do something like that again."

Suddenly Nancy heard a strange crackling noise. It was coming from her pocket.

"My walkie-talkie!" Nancy gasped. She pulled it out and held it to her ear. It crackled again. Then she heard a voice.

"Wow!" it said. "This is soooo totally cool!"

"Who are you?" Nancy shouted into the walkie-talkie. "Where's my walkie-talkie?"

Nancy heard a click. Then the walkie-talkie became silent.

"Who was that?" Bess asked. "Was it a boy or a girl?"

"Whoever it was," George said as she licked her ice-cream cone, "he or she has Nancy's walkie-talkie."

Nancy wrote down what the boy said.

"'Wow! This is sooo totally cool,'" Nancy repeated. "That's something Jason and Mike would say. Let's find them right now!"

The girls ran the few blocks to the Hutchings house. They ducked behind the fence as Jason walked out of his house and into the front yard.

Nancy, Bess, and George watched through the fence slats. Jason was leaning against a tree with something green in his hand. He pulled up what looked like an antenna. Then he began to speak into the green thing.

"Spaceship has landed on Planet Zonko," Jason called. "Craters are filled with guacamole dip."

Nancy's eyes opened wide.

"Bess, George," she whispered. "Jason has a green walkie-talkie!"

3

Meet Mystery Mouth

It's green," Bess whispered. "But are you sure it's a walkie-talkie?"

"Well, it isn't a dill pickle!" George said. She waved her cone in the air. "Let's get him!"

Nancy, Bess, and George ran out from behind the fence and straight to Jason.

He tucked the walkie-talkie under his arm as the girls surrounded him.

"Let me see that walkie-talkie, Jason," Nancy said, holding out her hand.

"No way!" Jason said. "Nothing will

loosen a Molehead's iron grip. What wimpy planet are you from?"

George grinned. She held her melting ice-cream cone right over Jason's head.

"The Big *Dripper!*" George exclaimed.

"Ahhh!" Jason yelled as sticky chocolate ice cream dripped over his head. As he reached up to cover his face, he dropped the walkie-talkie on the ground.

"Got it!" Nancy said. She was about to pick it up when she heard a loud yell.

She looked up and saw David and Mike charging toward them. They were wearing helmets, silver spacesuits, and matching space gloves. In David's hand was another green walkie-talkie.

How did they get *two*? Nancy wondered.

"Saved!" Jason cried. "By the *Moleheads from Mars* Space Patrol!"

"Ta-daaa!" David said. He held up his walkie-talkie. Splashed across the front were the words Space Patrol Radio.

Nancy looked down at the other walkie-talkie. It too had Space Patrol written on it. It wasn't her walkie-talkie at all.

"When did you get those?" George asked the boys.

David lifted his visor. "My mom bought me more than just school supplies today," he said. "Am I lucky or what?"

Nancy's heart sank. If the boys didn't have her walkie-talkie, who did?

"I just have one question," Nancy asked Jason. "Why did you and Mike leave the ice-cream truck without ice cream?"

"We had no more money," Mike said. "We'd spent the rest of our allowance on *Moleheads from Mars* cards."

"Let's go," George told Nancy and Bess. "There's no intelligent life on *this* planet."

"Stop!" David called as the girls turned to leave. "You have invaded our planet and tortured our leader!"

Nancy watched as David and Mike pointed their gloved fingers at the girls.

"Ready, aim—" David called.

"Oh, no!" Bess cried. "They're wearing space blaster squirt gloves!"

Nancy gulped. She had seen the gloves on a TV commercial.

"—fire!" Mike cried.

The girls shrieked as the boys squirted them with water. George dropped her ice-cream cone as they ran away.

"Stupid Moleheads!" Bess cried when they were safely away.

"You mean meatheads," George said.

Nancy shook water out of her reddish blond hair. Luckily her notebook hadn't gotten wet. She opened it and crossed out the boys' names.

"If it wasn't them," Bess asked, "then who was that mystery mouth?"

"Mystery Mouth!" Nancy giggled. "I like that. And that's what I'm going to call the culprit from now on."

Nancy and her friends agreed to meet the next day to look for more clues. After they said goodbye, Nancy went home.

Later at dinner she told her dad about the walkie-talkie. He wasn't angry, but he was very disappointed.

"Now we won't be able to use them at the mall on Saturday," Mr. Drew said.

"I'm sorry, Daddy," Nancy said. "I didn't think anyone would take it."

Hannah Gruen placed a steaming dish of

meatballs and spaghetti on the table. Hannah had been the Drews' housekeeper since Nancy was only three years old.

"Maybe no one took it," Hannah said. "It's a walkie-talkie. Maybe it just . . . walked away!"

Nancy giggled. Hannah always made her laugh.

"Somebody took it, Hannah." Nancy sighed. "Mystery Mouth already called me."

"Why don't you try to call him?" Mr. Drew asked Nancy. "He might be waiting for you to make the next move."

Nancy smiled. Mr. Drew was a lawyer. He always helped Nancy with her cases. And he always had good ideas.

"Okay, Daddy," Nancy said. She pulled the walkie-talkie from her pocket.

"Come in, come in," Nancy called. "Whoever you are."

Silence.

"He or she might be eating dinner," Hannah said. "Which is what *you* should be doing."

Nancy pictured her walkie-talkie at the boy's dinner table. Was Mystery Mouth

touching it with icky, sticky hands? Did he drop it in his soup bowl?

I've got to get it back, Nancy thought. No matter what!

That's when Nancy made herself a promise. Not only would she find her walkie-talkie, but she would find it by Saturday and take it to the mall.

After dinner Nancy ran straight to her room. Her chocolate Labrador puppy, Chocolate Chip, sat at her feet as she called into her walkie-talkie—over and over again.

"I have to get Mystery Mouth's attention, Chip," Nancy said. "But how?"

Nancy looked around the room. On her desk were a cassette player and tapes.

"That's it!" Nancy said. "I'll play some loud music. That'll stir him up!"

Nancy searched through her cassettes. She came across a tape of her favorite TV show, *Mr. Lizard's Funhouse.*

"Perfect!" Nancy said. "Mr. Lizard always plays wild music when he does the lizard dance."

Nancy placed the walkie-talkie and cassette player side by side. She popped the tape in and pressed Start. Then she turned the volume all the way up.

"Mr. Lizard—is a wizard—when it comes to fun—"

Nancy couldn't keep herself from doing the lizard dance. She hopped up and down, wiggled her fingers behind her head, and flicked out her tongue. Until . . .

"Hey! Hey!" a voice shouted. "Put a sock in it, will you?"

Chip barked at the walkie-talkie. Mystery Mouth had answered!

Nancy shut off the music. She held the walkie-talkie to her mouth.

"Are you there?" she asked.

"I'm here, I'm here," Mystery Mouth answered. "But you almost trashed my ears with that Mr. Lizard music. Ouch!"

"Who are you?" Nancy demanded.

"That's for me to know," Mystery Mouth said, "and for you to find out!"

Find out?

Nancy stared at the walkie-talkie. How would she do that?

4

Clue in the Castle

Give me a hint," Nancy said. "Are you a boy or a girl?"

"Nuh-uh," Mystery Mouth said. "My lips are sealed."

Nancy noticed something. Mystery Mouth was pronouncing his *s* letters like *th*. *Lips* sounded like *lipth*, and *sealed* sounded like *thealed*.

Nancy hadn't noticed that before. She'd have to remember to write the clue in her notebook.

"You didn't answer me when I called you before," Nancy said. "How come?"

"I must have been eating dinner," Mystery Mouth replied. "We had tuna casserole with melted cheese and—"

"I don't want to know what you had for dinner," Nancy interrupted. "All I want is my other walkie-talkie."

"What for?" Mystery Mouth joked. "I thought you girls just played with dolls."

Nancy's eyes lit up. Mystery Mouth had given her a clue. He was a boy!

"Give me back my walkie-talkie or you'll be in big trouble," Nancy said.

"Okay, okay," Mystery Mouth said. "You'll get your walkie-talkie."

"When?" Nancy asked. "How?"

The walkie-talkie became silent. Then Mystery Mouth began to whisper:

"Listen carefully because I'm only going to say this once."

"Say what?" Nancy asked.

"Tomorrow morning at eleven o'clock go to where the pirate ship meets the clown," Mystery Mouth said. "Look inside the castle tower for a big surprise."

Nancy wrinkled her nose. It sounded as if Mystery Mouth was giving her clues.

"Over and out," Mystery Mouth said.

Nancy heard a click, and the walkie-talkie went silent. She ran to her notebook and opened it. Then she wrote the words *pirate ship, castle,* and *clown.*

Pirate ship, castle, clown, Nancy thought. Where have I seen those things before?

Suddenly she remembered.

"The miniature golf course!" Nancy said to herself. "They have all kinds of things to hit the balls through. Like a pirate ship, a clown's mouth, and a castle with a tower!"

Nancy ran downstairs. She got permission to play miniature golf the next day. Then she called Bess and George. They got permission, too.

Maybe Mystery Mouth is going to leave my walkie-talkie inside the castle tower, Nancy thought. Or maybe it's just a trick.

The next morning at eleven o'clock Hannah drove Nancy, Bess, and George to the miniature golf course.

On the way Nancy filled her friends in on

her new clues. Like the way Mystery Mouth pronounced his *s* letters.

"Wow," Bess said. "He must have trouble saying 'She sells seashells by the seashore.'"

Nancy carried her walkie-talkie in the pocket of her denim jacket. She kept it turned on, just in case Mystery Mouth tried to reach her again.

"Are you going to play miniature golf with us, Hannah?" Nancy asked as they picked out their golf clubs and scorecard.

"I'd rather eat a miniature doughnut in the cafeteria," Hannah joked. "But I'll wave to you through the glass."

The girls walked to the gate leading to the golf course. A crowd of little kids stood waiting to go in. By the paper crowns on their heads, Nancy could tell it was a birthday party.

"We have to pass all those kids," George said. "The castle is all the way at the end of the course."

"Let's ask them nicely," Nancy said.

Nancy found the birthday girl. Pinned to

her frilly pink blouse was a big yellow button with the number 5 on it.

"Happy birthday," Nancy told the girl. "Can my friends and I please go ahead of you? We just need to—"

"No! No! No!" the girl shouted. She stamped her foot. "It's my birthday, and you have to wait your turn!"

A crowd of five-year-olds surrounded Nancy. They had scowls on their faces and chocolate all over their hands.

Nancy sighed. "Okay, okay."

"What are we going to do now?" Bess asked as the kids walked through the gate.

Nancy smiled and shrugged.

"It *is* a miniature golf course," Nancy said. "So let's play golf."

Nancy, Bess, and George played miniature golf behind the birthday party.

They shot balls through a lion's mouth, a cottage, and a spinning Ferris wheel. But Nancy couldn't keep her eyes off hole sixteen—the castle.

When they finally reached the castle, Nancy peeked inside the tower. She didn't find her walkie-talkie—only a note.

"What does it say, Nancy?" George asked as Nancy unfolded it.

Nancy looked at the note. The message was made up of tiny cut-up letters from magazines and newspapers. But the letters were all scrambled.

Nancy was about to try to unscramble the message when she heard a crackling noise in her pocket. It was her walkie-talkie.

Nancy pulled it out and listened.

"Did you find my first clue yet?" Mystery Mouth asked. "Did you? Did you?"

"First clue?" Nancy asked, surprised. "You mean there are more?"

"You bet!" Mystery Mouth said excitedly. "Now listen carefully because I'm only going to say it once."

Here we go again, Nancy thought.

"Wait until two o'clock," Mystery Mouth said. "Then look for a *book*. But don't forget to *whisper*."

Click.

"'Book' . . . 'whisper'. . . " Nancy repeated. Her eyes lit up. "The library! It has tons of books. And you have to whisper when you're there."

"Maybe Mystery Mouth wants you to find a special book," Bess said.

"And the scrambled message might tell us which one," Nancy said excitedly.

George held the message. The girls worked to unscramble the jumbled letters: ZGIMAAN LSIMANA.

They finally came up with the words AMAZING ANIMALS.

"That must be the book he wants us to find," Nancy said.

"Why a book?" George asked. "We want to find the walkie-talkie."

"There might be a message inside the book," Nancy said hopefully. "Telling us where to find the walkie-talkie."

Nancy wrote the new clues in her notebook. By the time the girls left with Hannah it was twelve-thirty.

Hannah treated them to a pizza lunch on Main Street. At two o'clock she walked them to the River Heights Library.

"I'll do some shopping and pick you up in a half an hour," Hannah promised.

Nancy, Bess, and George entered the library. They headed straight to the chil-

33

dren's room. Nancy typed AMAZING ANI-MALS into the computer. She held her breath until the listing came up.

"There it is!" Nancy whispered. She wrote the number of the book on a tiny piece of paper. Then she and her friends ran to the right shelf.

"Amazing Animals!" Nancy said in an excited whisper. She pulled the book out and flipped through it. A piece of paper fell out. Nancy picked up the paper. There in big letters was written, "GOTCHA!"

"Another trick," Bess mumbled.

Nancy's shoulders slumped. She was about to shut the book when—

Crackle-crackle-crackle!

"You fell for it!" Mystery Mouth shouted. "Am I the man or what?"

Nancy froze. Mystery Mouth was yelling—right in the library!

"Quiet, girls," a voice said.

Nancy turned around slowly. Mrs. Perry, the librarian, was standing behind them with her finger against her lips.

"It wasn't us," Nancy told Mrs. Perry. "It was Mystery Mouth. I mean—"

Mrs. Perry looked puzzled. It was no use trying to explain.

Nancy sighed. "Sorry, Mrs. Perry. It won't happen again."

Nancy placed the book back on the shelf. When they left the library, George grabbed the walkie-talkie.

"Listen carefully because I'm only going to say this once," George hissed. "Give Nancy her walkie-talkie, or she'll pour hot mushy oatmeal into your sneakers, once she finds out who you are!"

"But we've only started to play this game," Mystery Mouth said.

"Game?" Nancy gasped. She grabbed the walkie-talkie and spoke into it. "From now on you're going to play *my* game."

"Really?" Mystery Mouth said. "What game is that?"

"It's called find the boy who walked off with my walkie-talkie," Nancy declared. "And I'm going to win!"

5

Spies and Pizza Pies

Walkie-talkie, tape recorder," Nancy said for the third time that night. She glanced at the two gadgets on her night table. "Check . . . check."

It was nine o'clock. Nancy was lying in bed. But she wasn't reading a book the way she often did before falling asleep.

Nancy was waiting for Mystery Mouth to call. And this time she had a plan.

Nancy would record his next message on her tape recorder. Then she would play it back and listen for clues.

There was just one problem: It was getting late and Nancy was getting sleepy.

"Oh, well, Chip." Nancy sighed. "I'm sure even pests like Mystery Mouth don't stay up past their bedtime."

Chip yawned from Nancy's fluffy pink rug. That caused Nancy to yawn, too.

Her eyelids grew heavy, and her head fell gently back on her pillow. She could feel herself drifting off to sleep when—

"Yo! Yo! Are you there?"

"Huh?" Nancy blinked and sat up straight. It was Mystery Mouth!

Nancy quietly placed the walkie-talkie next to the tape recorder. Then she pressed the Record button.

"I wanted to tell you this crazy dream I just had," Mystery Mouth said. "I was playing Frisbee, and it turned out to be a giant ice-cream sandwich."

"Do you like ice cream?" Nancy asked. She wanted Mystery Mouth to keep talking.

"You bet," he answered.

"What flavor?" Nancy asked.

"Oh, no, you don't," Mystery Mouth

warned. "Now you're getting personal."

The walkie-talkie crackled again.

"Down, Jake!" she heard Mystery Mouth say. "I said, down, boy!"

"Who's Jake?" Nancy asked.

Silence. Then a click.

"Yes!" Nancy cheered under her breath. It was a good thing she'd forgotten to turn off her walkie-talkie!

Nancy rewound her tape and played back the message. She turned up the volume and heard a dog barking in the background.

Chip heard it, too. She wagged her tail and barked at the tape recorder.

Nancy smiled as she wrote her two new clues in her notebook.

"Mystery Mouth may be sneaky, Chip," Nancy said. "But he won't be a mystery for long!"

"Who has a dog named Jake?" George asked Nancy the next day.

It was Friday morning. Nancy, Bess, and George had gotten permission to ride their bikes together to Main Street.

"I don't know," Nancy said as they chained their bikes to a rack. "But I'm sure there's a way to find out."

The girls walked along Main Street. Nancy was wearing red shorts and a white T-shirt with two big pockets.

One pocket held her walkie-talkie. The other held her detective notebook.

"You *have* to find your walkie-talkie today, Nancy," Bess said. "It's Friday, and you said you'd find it by Saturday."

"I know." Nancy sighed. She reached in her pocket to make sure her walkie-talkie was turned on. She was running out of time—and maybe batteries.

Just then Nancy saw the Mr. Swirly Head truck parked at the corner.

"After what happened last time," Bess said sadly, "I don't think I can ever eat another Skyscraper again."

The girls decided to have pizza instead. They walked into Falco's Pizza Parlor. Nancy saw eight-year-old Rebecca Ramirez standing at the counter.

Rebecca was wearing a T-shirt from

Camp Curtain Up, a drama day camp. It was the perfect camp for her because she wanted to be an actress.

Nancy went up to her and said, "Hi, Rebecca. How do you like camp?"

"I love it!" Rebecca exclaimed. "I just got the part of the fairy godmother in *Cinderella!*"

Nancy jumped back as Rebecca sprinkled them with a stinky white powder.

"And so you shall!" Rebecca chanted. "And so you shall! And so you—"

"Quit it, Rebecca!" George cried. "That's not pixie dust—it's grated cheese!"

"What would you like, girls?" Mr. Falco asked from behind the counter.

"I'll have one plain slice, please," Nancy said. "And a medium—"

Crackle, crackle, crackle!

A voice piped up from Nancy's walkie-talkie: "Pizza rocks! Yum, yum, yum!"

Nancy froze. How did Mystery Mouth know she was in the pizza parlor? Unless he was in the pizza parlor, too, and spying on her.

Nancy spun around. She stared at the

other customers. "Bess," she said. "Were any of these people in the ice-cream line the other day?"

"I don't know!" Bess wailed. "Maybe if they were eating ice cream instead of pizza, I'd be able to tell."

"Will someone please tell me what's going on here?" Rebecca demanded.

"And will someone please tell *me* what you girls are ordering?" Mr. Falco said. "I don't have all day."

The four friends ordered their slices. They carried their trays to a table under a leafy hanging plant.

While they ate, Nancy told Rebecca all about her new case and her clues.

"Mystery Mouth has a dog named Jake," Nancy said. "He likes ice cream. And he pronounces his *s* words like a *th*. Like ithe cream and Frithbee."

"I did that once," Rebecca said. "When I lost my two front teeth."

"Nancy!" George gasped. "Do you think Mystery Mouth has no front teeth?"

"It's possible," Nancy said.

"Yay!" Bess cheered. "Now all we have to

do is find a boy with two missing front teeth. That should be easy."

"Yeah." Nancy sighed. "If you're the tooth fairy."

Rebecca dropped her pizza on her paper plate. "I'll be your tooth fairy, Nancy!" she exclaimed.

"Rebecca, I was only kidding," Nancy said with a smile.

"I'm not!" Rebecca said. "I'll dress up in my fairy godmother costume and give cookies to all the kids with no front teeth. It'll be great practice for my starring role!"

"And we can hide nearby and listen for Mystery Mouth's voice," George added.

"And Rebecca can make everyone say 'She sells seashells by the seashore,'" Bess said. "It's hard to say that without front teeth."

Nancy thought about it. The idea was so weird that it might work.

"Well, Nancy?" Rebecca asked. "What do you say?"

"I say, watch out, Mystery Mouth," Nancy said. "Because the truth might be in the *tooth!*"

6

Tooth or Dare

Bess!" George scolded. "Those cookies are for the tooth fairy!"

"Mmmph," Bess mumbled. Her cheeks were puffed out, and her mouth was covered with crumbs.

Nancy stepped back. She looked at the table that she, Bess, and George had set up in front of Rebecca's house.

On it was a big plate of oatmeal cookies, a bowl of blue and green glitter, and a sign that read Meet the Tooth Fairy, 2:30.

"Here I am!" Rebecca sang as she ran out

of her house to the table. She was wearing a party dress, and a sparkly tiara was in her hair. "I had to look all over my room for my magic wand."

"Why do you need a magic wand?" Nancy asked.

Rebecca waved her wand. "Because when I find the boy who took your walkie-talkie, I'm going to turn him into a toad."

"Rebecca, you're the tooth fairy," George said. "Just give him a cavity."

Nancy looked at her watch. It was twenty minutes after two.

"Places, everybody," Nancy said. She turned to Rebecca. "Now, remember. Don't give cookies to everyone. Just those with missing front teeth."

"I know, I know." Rebecca sighed. "It was my idea."

Nancy turned off her walkie-talkie. She didn't want anyone to hear Mystery Mouth if he suddenly called. Then she, Bess, and George hid behind a tree.

Peeking out, Nancy could see Rebecca sit

down behind the table. She waved her magic wand and began to shout:

"Show me your missing teeth! And you'll get a big treat!"

Nancy saw a boy ride over on his bicycle. He smiled to show his missing front teeth. Then he reached for a cookie.

"Wait!" Rebecca said. "First you have to say 'She sells seashells by the seashore' three times fast."

"Okay," the boy said. "Thee thells theethells by the—"

Rebecca shrieked. The boy was spitting all over her.

"Hey!" Rebecca shouted. "Say it, don't spray it!"

The boy grabbed a cookie and rode away.

"Was he the one?" George whispered.

"No," Nancy whispered back. "That boy sounded too young."

Nancy watched as a six-year-old girl walked to the table.

"Show me your teeth and you'll get a big treat!" Rebecca sang out.

"Here!" the girl said. She dropped a tooth on the table. "It just fell out."

"Ewww!" Rebecca cried.

"You're the tooth fairy, aren't you?" the girl asked. She picked up a cookie. "Deal with it."

"Wow," Bess whispered to Nancy. "I didn't realize the tooth fairy had such a gross job!"

The girls waited. Soon more kids were lining up at the table.

"Mystery Mouth has got to be in that line," Nancy said hopefully.

"Look who else is there," George groaned. "Lonny and Lenny Wong."

Nancy gulped. Lonny and Lenny were six-year-old twins. They were also pests.

"Show me your teeth and you'll get a big treat," Rebecca said.

"Forget the cookies," Lonny said, waving his hand. "We want quarters."

"Yeah!" Lenny said. "We always get a quarter from the tooth fairy. So pay up!"

Rebecca planted her hands on her hips. "Today I'm giving out cookies," she said. "Take them or leave them."

"Okay," Lonny said. He took a cookie. "But only because I like chocolate chips."

"Those aren't chocolate chip," Rebecca said as Lonny bit into the cookie. "They're oatmeal."

Lonny's eyes opened wide. He clapped his hand over his mouth.

"Now you did it," Lenny told Rebecca. "Lonny *hates* oatmeal cookies."

"Phooey!" Lonny spat. "Phooey! Phooey! Phooey! Phooooo—"

"Stop!" Rebecca yelled. "You're spitting cookie crumbs all over me!"

"And all over the cookies," a boy said. "I'm not eating those cookies now."

"Yuck! Me neither," a girl said.

Nancy watched as all the kids walked away. "Great," she said. "Now we'll never get to check out those kids."

Nancy, Bess, and George walked out from behind the tree. Rebecca was covered with glitter, spit, and crumbs.

"Whose dumb idea was this anyway?" Rebecca demanded.

"Yours!" Nancy, Bess, and George answered at the same time.

Nancy, Bess, and George helped Rebecca

carry the table and chair into her house. After saying goodbye to Rebecca, the girls left the Ramirez house.

"What do we do now?" Nancy asked as they climbed on their bikes.

"I say we go to Andrew Leoni's house," George said, "and question him."

"I still don't think it was Andrew," Nancy said.

"Then who was it?" Bess asked. "And who has a dog named Jake?"

Nancy didn't know any dogs named Jake. But she did know someone who might.

"Bess, George!" Nancy said. "Chip's veterinarian knows lots of dogs in River Heights. He might be able to tell us who owns a dog named Jake."

The girls gave each other high fives. Then they rode their bikes around the corner to Dr. Rios's office.

"May I help you?" the desk nurse asked as the girls walked in.

"Yes," Nancy said. "Are any of your patients named Jake?"

The nurse entered something on her computer. "There *is* a pet named Jake," she said. "And he just had a checkup on Wednesday afternoon at four-thirty."

"Yes!" Nancy cheered.

"But I don't think he's the pet you're looking for," the nurse added.

"Why not?" Nancy asked.

The door slammed open. Nancy saw their friend Katie Zaleski run into the office with her parrot, Lester, in her arms.

"Help!" Katie cried. "Lester just swallowed a hot chili pepper! Now his feathers are all ruffled!"

"Hot stuff, hot stuff," Lester squawked. "Arr—rrrk!"

The nurse jumped up. She led Katie into the doctor's office.

"Poor Katie," Bess said.

"I hope Lester is okay," Nancy said.

"Hey, you guys!" George called. "Check it out!"

Nancy spun around. George was standing behind the nurse's computer.

"Guess who has a pet named Jake?" George asked.

"Who?" Nancy and Bess asked at the same time.

George pointed to the computer. "Andrew Leoni!"

7

Jake Takes the Cake

Are you sure it's Andrew?" Nancy asked.

"See for yourself," George said. "It's Andrew's last name. And his address on Tide Street."

Nancy was about to look at the computer screen. Then the nurse stepped out of Dr. Rios's office.

"I'm sorry, girls," the nurse said. "The information on our computer is personal."

"We just want to know more about Jake, please," Nancy said.

The phone on the nurse's desk rang.

"Hello?" the nurse answered. She looked surprised. "Your cat did what?"

The nurse looked busy, so the girls left the office.

"Now will you write Andrew's name in your book?" George asked Nancy.

"I guess." Nancy sighed. She opened her detective notebook and wrote Andrew's name. Underneath she wrote: "Probably in ice-cream line. Has a pet named Jake. Saw doctor on Wednesday, 4:30."

But Nancy still wasn't sure.

"How do we know if Andrew has a *dog* named Jake?" Nancy asked. "The pet on the computer might have been a cat."

"Cats have names like Fluffy or Snowball," Bess said. "Not Jake."

Nancy shut her notebook.

"Then let's go to Andrew's house right now," she said. "We'll check out Jake. Then we'll ask Andrew to say 'She sells seashells at the seashore.'"

The girls jumped on their bikes and pedaled to Tide Street. Nancy knew the Leoni house. She had seen Andrew playing in his yard many times.

Why didn't I ever see a dog, too? Nancy wondered.

The girls walked up to the front door. Nancy rang the doorbell. Andrew looked surprised when he opened the door.

"Hey," Andrew said. "What's up?"

Nancy didn't want to ask about Jake right away. She knew that a good detective always led up to the big question.

"Do you know what some people call the hottest days of August?" Nancy asked.

"Is this a quiz?" Andrew asked. "Because school doesn't start for another three weeks, four days, and fifteen hours."

George looked at her watch. "Sixteen," she corrected.

"It's not a quiz, Andrew," Nancy said with a smile. "More like a riddle."

"I like riddles," Andrew said. He scratched his chin as he thought. "Let's see . . . the hottest days of August . . ."

Nancy stared at Andrew's pockets. She saw the outline of something in one. It was the same size and shape as her walkie-talkie.

"I know!" Andrew cried. "They call them

scorchers. That's what the weatherman called one day last week. A scorcher!"

"Wrong," Nancy said. "They're called the dog days of August. *Dog* days!"

Andrew shrugged. "So?"

"So—do you have a dog named Jake?" Nancy blurted.

"And did you take Nancy's walkie-talkie?" Bess demanded.

"Come clean, Andrew," George snapped. "We know all about the stamps."

Andrew looked really confused now.

"I don't have any walkie-talkies," he said. "And I don't have a dog named Jake."

"Then why did you go to Dr. Rios's office on Tuesday?" Nancy asked. "Four-thirty, to be exact?"

Andrew rolled his eyes.

"Du-uh!" he said. "Because I have a rat named Jake."

Nancy gulped. "A . . . rat?"

Bess shrieked as a gray rat scurried around Andrew's feet onto the doorstep.

"Rats make awesome pets," Andrew said. "This one even loves Coco-Cakes."

Andrew reached into his pocket. He pulled out a package of cream-filled cupcakes and ripped it open.

So that's what was in his pocket, Nancy thought.

Andrew took a bite. Then he bent over and offered some to Jake. The rat stood on its hind legs and nibbled the cupcake.

"Gross!" the girls cried at the same time. They spun around on their heels and ran to their bikes.

"We forgot to ask Andrew to say 'She sells seashells,'" Bess said as they ran.

"It's okay," Nancy said. "Andrew is no longer a suspect."

"Because he has a rat?" George asked.

"No," Nancy said. She stopped running and opened her notebook. "Because he wasn't in the pizza parlor when I got that message. And he used his front teeth to bite that cupcake."

Then Nancy noticed something else.

"Hey!" Nancy said. "The nurse said that Jake's checkup was Wednesday at four-thirty. That's when my walkie-talkie was taken."

Nancy pointed to where she had written the time and day in her notebook.

"I guess Andrew is innocent," George said.

Nancy crossed Andrew's name out in her notebook. She was glad he didn't take her walkie-talkie. She liked Andrew, even if he did feed cupcakes to his rat.

"Now I have zero suspects," Nancy said as she shut her book. "And Mystery Mouth hasn't called all day."

The girls climbed up on their bikes. Bess giggled when her stomach growled. It was getting close to dinnertime.

"I guess we'll have to look for more clues tomorrow," George said.

Nancy's heart sank. Tomorrow was Saturday. She had promised to find her walkie-talkie by then.

The three friends said goodbye. Then Nancy rode her bike home.

During dinner Nancy could hardly eat her fried chicken. She was too worried about her walkie-talkie. After excusing herself from the table, Nancy went outside. She began brushing Chip in her front yard.

"I may never hear from Mystery Mouth again, Chip," Nancy said as she brushed. "What if—"

CRACKLE, CRACKLE, CRACKLE!

Nancy almost dropped the brush. She was getting a signal on her walkie-talkie!

Chip whined while Nancy pulled the walkie-talkie from her pocket.

She was about to say something, but Mystery Mouth beat her to it.

"Your dog is way cool!" he piped up. "But my dog is way bigger."

Mystery Mouth is watching me! Nancy thought. Her eyes darted around the yard.

She gasped when she saw a bright blue shape bobbing over the row of hedges.

"Who's there?" Nancy called as she ran to the hedge. The shape disappeared.

Nancy wanted to peek over the hedge, but it was too tall. And she wasn't allowed to leave the yard after dinner.

"What was that, Chip?" Nancy asked slowly. "And where have I seen it before?"

8

Pop Goes the Quiz

What good is one walkie-talkie?" Nancy asked herself the next morning. She stared down at the walkie-talkie in her hand. "It's like having one roller skate."

It was Saturday morning. Nancy was sitting on her front doorstep. In just one hour she and her dad would go to the mall—without her set of walkie-talkies.

Nancy heard footsteps. Was it the mysterious blue thing again?

She glanced up and saw Bess and George walking into her yard.

61

"Hi, Nancy," George said. "We wanted to see how you were doing."

"And if you had any new clues," Bess added.

Nancy told her friends all about the mysterious message the night before. And the blue thing behind the hedge.

"It was sort of like a blob," Nancy explained. "A bright blue blob."

"A blob!" George gasped. "Maybe it was a creature from outer space."

"George!" Bess complained. "You're beginning to sound like the boys."

CRACKLE! CRACKLE! CRACKLE!

Nancy glared at her walkie-talkie. Mystery Mouth was back. And this time she wanted answers.

"Who are you?" Nancy demanded. "Tell me right now!"

"Nah," Mystery Mouth answered. "That would spoil all the fun."

"Fun?" Nancy cried. But then she heard music in the background.

She waved Bess and George over to listen. Then she placed her hand over the walkie-talkie.

"What tune is that?" Nancy whispered.

"I'm not sure," Bess whispered back. "But it's making my mouth water."

Nancy stared at Bess. Her mouth always watered when she heard the Mr. Swirly Head jingle.

"It's the Mr. Swirly Head truck!" Nancy said.

"Nancy!" George said. "Could Mystery Mouth be standing by the ice-cream truck?"

Nancy put the pieces together. Mr. Swirly Head . . . blue blob . . . .

"That's it!" she cried. "I just remembered where I saw that blue thing before. On Ethan Taylor's head!"

"Ethan?" Bess asked.

Nancy shut off her walkie-talkie so Mystery Mouth wouldn't hear. "He was wearing a blue plastic swirly hat in the ice-cream truck!" she said.

"What makes you think he took your walkie-talkie?" George asked.

"The Mr. Swirly Head truck was parked outside the pizza parlor when I got that weird message," Nancy remembered. "He must have seen us go inside."

"But I don't remember Ethan having a missing tooth," George said.

"Me neither," Nancy said. "But we have to find the Mr. Swirly Head truck!"

"Where is it?" Bess asked.

Nancy saw a boy with red hair walk past her house. He was holding a chocolate Skyscraper.

George blew her soccer whistle. "Hey, you!" she called. "Stop! Wait up!"

The boy looked confused as Nancy and her friends ran over to him.

"Please!" Nancy said. "Tell us where the Mr. Swirly Head truck is."

The boy took a long lick of his cone. "It's somewhere on Cherry Street," he said.

"That's only two blocks away," Nancy told Bess and George. "Let's hurry!"

"Wow!" the boy called as the girls ran down the block. "You must want ice cream really bad!"

Nancy, Bess, and George ran the two blocks to Cherry Street. Sure enough, the Mr. Swirly Head truck was parked in the middle of the block.

There were three kids in line. Nancy saw

Mr. Swirly Head lean out of the truck with an ice-cream bar. He was wearing his pink swirly hat again.

"There's Mr. Swirly Head," Nancy said. "But I don't see Ethan."

"Maybe he's not helping his father in the truck today," George said. She twirled the soccer whistle between her fingers.

Nancy stared at George's soccer whistle. She got an idea.

"There's one way to find out," Nancy said. She grabbed George's whistle and blew into it hard.

TWEEEEEEEE!!!

"Yow!" a voice yelled from the truck. A hot-fudge sundae flew out of the window.

"Hey!" a kid in line shouted as he jumped back.

Nancy watched as a bright blue swirl rose slowly in the truck window.

"It's Ethan!" Nancy cried.

The girls excused themselves as they ran past the kids to the window.

"H-hi, Nancy," Ethan stammered.

As he smiled nervously, Nancy could see he was missing a front tooth.

"Hi, Mystery Mouth," Nancy said. "Now may I please have my walkie-talkie back?"

"What walkie-talkie?" Ethan asked.

Nancy looked into the truck. She saw Mr. Swirly Head making a vanilla Skyscraper. Then she saw a picture of a dog taped to the ice-cream machine.

Nancy looked closer. The dog was eating from a dish marked Jake.

"You have a dog named Jake!" Nancy declared.

"So?" Ethan asked.

Nancy heard the crackling noise. But this time it wasn't coming from her pocket—it was coming from Ethan's.

Ethan turned red as he clapped his hand over his pocket. Nancy could see a green antenna sticking out.

"There it is!" Nancy cried. "I'll bet that's my walkie-talkie!"

Mr. Swirly Head walked over. "What's this about a walkie-talkie, Ethan?" he asked. "You told us you didn't find one."

"I didn't, Dad!" Ethan said.

Nancy frowned. Was Ethan lying?

"I didn't find it until after the girls left,"

Ethan went on. "It was in the Frozen Swirly Bars bin. At first I thought it was a Lime Ricky Ticky."

"Why didn't you give it right back?" Nancy asked. "You knew it belonged to me."

"I was going to," Ethan said. "But first I wanted to come up with some clues."

"Clues?" Bess cried. "Why?"

"So I could see if the best detective really was the best," Ethan said.

Nancy couldn't believe her ears. All this time Ethan was testing her to see if she was a good detective!

"Well?" George asked with a grin. "Is Nancy the best detective?"

Ethan pulled the green walkie-talkie from his pocket. He handed it to Nancy.

"She sure is!" he said.

Nancy smiled with relief. But she was still angry with Ethan.

"Your game might have been fun for you," Nancy said. "But it wasn't for me."

"Nancy's right, Ethan," Mr. Swirly Head said. "And she deserves an apology."

"Say it, Ethan," George urged.

"Yeah, say it," a girl in line called. "So we can have our ice cream!"

"Okay, okay." Ethan sighed. "I'm sorry, Nancy."

"Apology accepted," Nancy said. "I just have one more question."

"What?" Ethan asked.

"When did you lose your front tooth?" Nancy asked with a smile.

"Right after I found your walkie-talkie," Ethan said. "On a frozen Lime Ricky Ticky. It was loose anyway."

"Now I hope you girls will accept three free ice-cream cones," Mr. Swirly Head said.

"Skyscrapers?" Bess gasped.

"The sky's the limit!" Mr. Swirly Head said with a grin.

While Ethan handed ice-cream bars to the other kids, Mr. Swirly Head made three Skyscrapers. Vanilla for Nancy. Chocolate for George. Strawberry for Bess.

Nancy knew her Skyscraper would taste awesome. Ice cream always tasted best after she'd solved a case.

"So, Bess," Nancy said. "Do you still want to see how my walkie-talkies work?"

"No, thanks," Bess said with a smile. "I think I already know!"

Later that day Nancy and her dad went to the mall. Nancy picked out a red fleece jacket, a denim skirt, and brown loafers.

Nancy didn't get lost. But now she had both walkie-talkies—just in case.

While Mr. Drew drove the car home, Nancy wrote in her detective notebook:

I love my new school clothes. But most of all I love having *two* walkie-talkies. I guess I kind of expected to solve this case. What I *didn't* expect was a pop quiz!

And since school starts in just three weeks, three days, and sixteen and a half hours—I'd better get used to it.

Case closed—over and out!

EASY TO READ—FUN TO SOLVE!

**Meet up with suspense and mystery
in The Hardy Boys® are:**

THE CLUES™
BROTHERS

Available from Minstrel® Books
Published by Pocket Books

2389

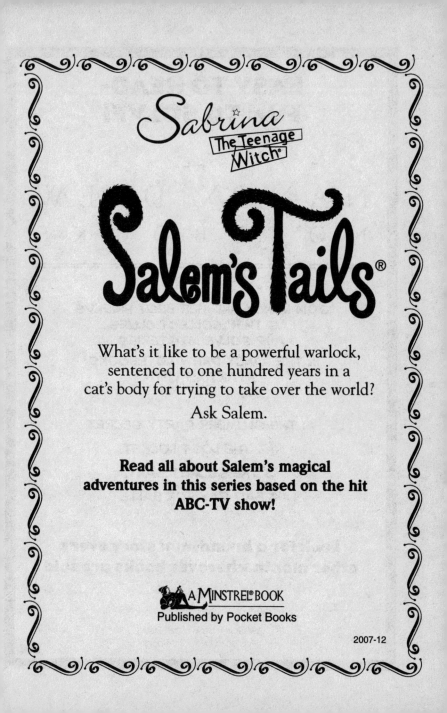

Sabrina
The Teenage Witch®

Salem's Tails®

What's it like to be a powerful warlock,
sentenced to one hundred years in a
cat's body for trying to take over the world?
Ask Salem.

**Read all about Salem's magical
adventures in this series based on the hit
ABC-TV show!**

A MINSTREL® BOOK
Published by Pocket Books

2007-12